Brot... W...

Characters

Tom

Kim

Mike

John

Bells

Setting

A bedroom, early in the morning

Picture Words

bells

morning

Sight Words

are	get	I	is
it	to	up	you

ringing

sleeping

Enrichment Words

brother

late

talk

time

Tom: John! John!

Kim: Brother John.

Mike: Are you sleeping?

John: Yes, I am sleeping.

Mike: No, you are not sleeping. You can not talk when you are sleeping.

Tom: John! John!

Kim: Brother John.

Mike: It is time to get up. Get out of bed.

John: I want to sleep.

Mike: It is morning.
Can you hear the bells?

Bells: We ring. Ding, ding, dong!

Ding, ding, dong!

Kim: Bells!

Tom: I hear the bells.

Mike: The morning bells are ringing.

Bells: We ring. Ding, ding, dong.

Tom: John! John!

Kim: Brother John.

Mike: It is time to get up!

Bells: Ding, ding, dong.

Tom: We must go.
We will be late.

Bells: Ding, ding, dong.
Ding, ding, dong.

John: Okay! I hear the bells. I will get up.

The End